Love Puppies

WE'RE HERE TO HELP!

The Fast and the Furriest

JaNay Brown-Wood

SCHOLASTIC INC.

To all the Small-But-Mighties out there.
Remember, you are POWERFUL!

Copyright © 2024 by JaNay Brown-Wood.

Interior illustrations by Eric Proctor, © 2024 Scholastic Inc.

All rights reserved. Published by Scholastic Inc., *Publishers since 1920.* SCHOLASTIC and associated logos are trademarks and/or registered trademarks of Scholastic Inc.

The publisher does not have any control over and does not assume any responsibility for author or third-party websites or their content.

No part of this publication may be reproduced, stored in a retrieval system, or transmitted in any form or by any means, electronic, mechanical, photocopying, recording, or otherwise, without written permission of the publisher. For information regarding permission, write to Scholastic Inc., Attention: Permissions Department, 557 Broadway, New York, NY 10012.

This book is a work of fiction. Names, characters, places, and incidents are either the product of the author's imagination or are used fictitiously, and any resemblance to actual persons, living or dead, business establishments, events, or locales is entirely coincidental.

ISBN 978-1-339-04217-6

10 9 8 7 6 5 4 3 2 1   24 25 26 27 28

Printed in the U.S.A.   40

First printing 2024

Book design by Omou Barry

Decorative design border art © Shutterstock.com

Fall in love with each paw-fectly sweet adventure!

TABLE OF CONTENTS

Chapter 1
New to the Crew

"Two words!" shouted Noodles, Rosie, and Clyde all together as Barkley held up his two paws. Barkley nodded then lowered one.

"First word," called Rosie.

Barkley nodded again and his paw pads

began to glow bright purple. He was magical! A dachshund with the power to transform into almost anything—and even disappear or camouflage, too. At that moment, his belly started to stretch so that it was as long and skinny as a string. Then he jiggled his tummy around and around.

"Jump rope! It's a jump rope," giggled Rosie.

Barkley shook his head, jiggling some more. Then he snapped his teeth at the air as if eating something.

"String cheese?" called Clyde, the Shar-Pei, floating up into the air to get a better look. Clyde was magical, too. The whole Love Puppy crew was!

Clyde's magic was the ability to fly. He could also taste things in the air from at least a mile away.

Barkley shook his head again.

"Oh, I know," called Noodles. "You're a noodle."

Barkley yipped with excitement, then held up his other paw. He shrank his body down, down, down to a Jar-Barkley.

"Gravy?" called Clyde.

"Noodle sauce?" said Noodles.

"I know! You're spaghetti sauce," shouted Rosie.

"You got it," said Barkley, morphing back into his puppy body.

"Wooohooo," said Rosie, tossing rose petals into

the air. She had flower magic, which allowed her to grow flowers and plants wherever she was.

"That was paw-some," said Noodles, who sent a breeze through the Doghouse, their Love Puppy Headquarters, and caused Rosie's flower petals to swirl around all her puppy teammates. Noodles could control elements of the weather. She was also *really* good at reading strong emotions in the room.

All their magical powers came in handy when they were on special Love Puppy missions to help human children! They had just completed their last mission and it was another great success!

So then and there in the Love Puppy living room, the puppy team played, yipped, and laughed. Even the banner-pups joined in on the fun. They were animated versions of the Love Puppies, but on a flag that matched each Love Puppy's signature color: pink for Rosie, orange for Noodles, purple for Barkley, and blue for Clyde.

Noodles looked toward the banner-pups and blew another happy breeze causing each banner to sway and flap.

"Who's up next?" asked Barkley.

"Me, me, meee," called Clyde, zooming to take Barkley's place at the front of the room.

Just then, a strange chiming melody began

to play. Somewhere in the room, loud chimes twinkled and twanged.

"What's that noise?" asked Noodles, looking all around. None of the pups recognized it.

"Wait! It's coming from the Crystal Bone," said Barkley. "Look!"

Each of the pups turned their attention toward the large crystalline bone that stood in the corner. Usually, it buzzed and floated when there was a new mission for the pups to solve, flashing each of their signature colors. With Rosie's touch, it would reveal what human the pups would need to help today.

But this time, the Bone was planted firmly on

the ground. The chiming melody played from it like a wind chime in a storm. It did flash, though, repeating the new pattern over and over again: pink, orange, purple, blue, gold. Pink, orange, purple, blue, gold.

"You've never played that song before, Bone," Rosie said as she padded across the living room toward it. The other pups hurried to join her. "What is it? What are you trying to tell us?" she asked.

"Maybe Bone's broken," said Clyde "and it forgot how to tell us we have a mission."

"I'm not sure this new song is for a mission at all," said Rosie.

"Could it be for a mission we have to revisit?"

asked Noodles. "Like maybe we have to help a kid we've already helped!"

"Like Caleb or Eliana?" said Barkley.

"Or Jayden? Or maybe Magnolia?" said Clyde.

"Or what if it's Jasmine and Meiko who need us again?" added Barkley. He and Clyde hugged each other, their tails wagging furiously with worry.

"Hold on, Pups," said Rosie. "No need to fret just yet. I bet Bone will tell us everything we need to know. Let's find out for sure."

Rosie turned and faced the Crystal Bone and placed her paws on the slick, crystal surface. The Bone flashed three times and a video projected onto the ceiling.

"Hello, Love Puppies," said a man's voice in an English accent.

"Bone, you can speak?" said Barkley.

"Bone's always been able to speak," said Rosie. "How do you think it would tell me about all the missions? Oh, I guess it was only me who could hear Bone before."

"Yes, Pups," continued the Bone. "I have exciting news to tell you, which is why I am addressing all of you instead of just Rosie."

The Bone flashed again and a video of the pups helping on all their past missions played across the ceiling.

"You pups have done an amazing job helping

human children in need. Each and every one of the kids from your past missions is thriving and doing fantastically well," said the Bone.

"Yip yip HOORAY!" called Rosie.

"Way to go, Pups," called Noodles.

"That's pup-tastic," yipped Barkley with excitement as he and Clyde did a happy jig.

"As of today, your duties are going to grow," continued the Bone.

"Doo-dees," laughed Clyde.

"Focus, silly pup," giggled Rosie.

"You pups will continue to help more humans in need. But now I have added a new element. Sometimes, I will also send you a new Love Puppy pal who you will train to help others. You will show this new puppy what you do: how you help kids, how you solve your problems, and how you spread love and joy everywhere you go."

"We can definitely do that," yipped Noodles.

"No doggie-doubt about it!" added Clyde.

"Congratulations on being such a pup-tastic team!" said the Bone. Light then flashed across the room, like confetti falling from the ceiling. The banner-pups yipped and danced on their fabrics, and the Love Puppy team hugged and celebrated. It was nice to know that all their hard work was really paying off!

"Wait! Look at that!" said Barkley, pointing

toward the banners hanging from the ceiling.

"I didn't even see that before," said Clyde. He zoomed up so he was eye level with a golden banner that now hung beside the others. "A new banner. But it's empty!"

Just then, a sound came from the front door.

The puppies shared excited looks before they dashed from the living room to the front door. The golden banner sparkled and shimmered as a brand-new puppy appeared.

Chapter 2
Mission Samnang

"Who is it? Who is it?" called Clyde as the pups made it to the door.

Barkley opened it wide. There, right on the doormat, was a wicker basket.

"It's just a basket," said Barkley. "I don't see any new puppies here."

Then a tiny whimper came from the basket and the blanket inside wiggled ever so slightly. Barkley approached the basket cautiously with the rest of the team behind him. With his gentle paw, he pushed the blanket aside.

Inside was the tiniest puppy the team had ever seen. It was a baby corgi, with brown and white splotches all over its body. It also had a light brown patch around its eyes and a white stripe that went from the tip of its bright pink nose, all the way to the back of its head. The little newborn puppy wiggled and squeaked with its eyes tightly shut.

"It's like a squishy potato with spots all over it," said Clyde.

"You're not going to try to eat it, right?" asked Noodles with a grin.

"No way," said Clyde. "I already ate lunch!"

Barkley stepped closer. He sniffed the tiny puppy. When he moved his nose close, the puppy nuzzled right up to him.

"Awwww, it's so cute!" squealed Rosie.

"And so tiny. I hope we get to keep it forever," said Noodles.

At that moment, the Bone sounded off with its usual notification that a new mission was about to begin.

"Let's get this tiny pup inside," said Barkley. His body began to morph—his neck stretching upward and his tummy and legs turning into a rectangle.

"After you, Crane Truck-Barkley," said Rosie.

Mini Crane Truck-Barkley lifted the basket and then rolled inside in the direction of the Bone's vibrating and flashing.

"What's his name?" asked Clyde.

"Do we even know if it's a girl or a boy?" asked Noodles.

"I wonder what its powers are," added Rosie.

The pups crowded all around the basket as the Bone buzzed and flashed louder and brighter.

Noodles gently lifted the puppy. "Boy," she said. "It's definitely a boy!"

The Bone buzzed and flashed full blast.

"Uh-oh," said Rosie, finally turning to face it. "I think we'd better get focused on our new mission."

With the puppy resting in Noodles's lap, Rosie placed her paw onto the Bone and shut her eyes. "We're ready, Bone." Rosie's paw pads glowed pink as the Bone projected words onto the ceiling:

NAME: SAMNANG SOK
Age: Eight
Grade: Second
Problem: Kids being mean to him at school

"This is Samnang," said Rosie with her paws still touching the Bone. "He's in second grade. He's the oldest in his class, but the smallest."

A video flashed across the Bone's smooth surface. The pups watched as Samnang played with a bunch of kids that looked just like him. They laughed and kicked the ball around a field at the park. Samnang made a goal and all the kids celebrated, some rubbing his head, some squeezing his cheeks. Samnang smiled widely.

"He's got a bunch of family members, but none go to school with him," said Rosie.

The video changed and Samnang stood on a stage with a number clipped to his chest. A banner that said SPELLING BEE was behind him and people watched from the audience. Samnang said something into a microphone, and then confetti and balloons began to fall all around him. Everybody clapped, except for two boys in the front row, who also wore numbers attached to their shirts. The boys glared up at him.

"Yikes," said Barkley. "Those boys didn't seem too happy about Samnang winning."

The Bone flashed again, and this time, a hologram displayed right above it. The pups could see Samnang walking down a hallway, smiling. Then the two boys from the other video stepped in front of him. They yelled into Samnang's face and messed up his hair. "You only won because Ms. Chin likes you," said one, viciously.

All the pups gasped in horror.

"Oh no! Pups," said Rosie, "and there's more! Bone says this is happening RIGHT NOW! We don't have any time to lose. Paws in!"

Just then, the tiny puppy on Noodles's lap sneezed. The pups all snapped their heads in his direction, reminded that they had company.

"What about this little guy?" asked Barkley. "We can't just leave him, can we?"

"No way. He's too small to be by himself," said Noodles. "Should we take him with us?"

"What if he gets lost?" asked Clyde.

The pups had already had an experience with lost pets—like Caleb's Maxie. They definitely didn't want something like that to happen again. Especially not to them!

"And with how important this mission is, we need the *whole* team to attack this one," said Rosie.

But time was ticking away, and something was happening to poor Samnang right then!

What in the world would the puppies do now?

Chapter 3
A Boy and Two Bullies

Each of the Love Puppies looked at their tiny, new

teammate.

"Well, you did say we need our *whole* team," said

Barkley. "I guess that means this little guy as well."

The other pups nodded in agreement.

"It seems like our decision is made!" said Rosie. "This small dude is coming with us. We'll just have to be sure to keep an extra eye on him. You got the pooch, Pup?" she asked, looking Barkley's way.

With that, Barkley's tummy morphed into a puppy cushion with his head, tail, and legs still attached. He wrapped his legs snuggly around the puppy, like a hug. "Got the pooch," he said.

"In that case, paws in!" said Rosie.

Each of the puppies—except for the tiny one— placed their paws in the center of their huddle, their paw pads glowing brightly.

"With the power of love, anything is paw-sible! Love Puppies, go!"

WHOOSH!

* * *

The pups landed next to a shrub outside an open window. They all looked inside to see a school hallway.

"Whoa," said Barkley. "Look at this guy. It's like he grew in the last couple of minutes or something."

It was true. The little potato-sized puppy was now the size of a small pumpkin, and his eyes were wide open. He sniffed around. Then he wagged his tail and dropped his tongue out like he was happy to see the other pups.

"Well, look at you—" started Rosie, but just then, hushed voices bounced off the hallway walls.

"There he is," Noodles whispered. "There's Samnang!"

Sure enough, there, pushed up against the wall, was Samnang. And there, too, were the same two boys from before. They towered over Samnang, crowding in his face. The blond one had a finger pointed right at Samnang's nose, and the other balled up his right fist and hit it into his own open palm.

"Oh no! Oh no!" whimpered Rosie.

"What do we do, Rosie?" cried Noodles. "What do we do?"

"We've got to help him!" cried Clyde.

"Poor Samnang," said Barkley, who still held

the baby puppy tightly. "See him, little pup?" said Barkley into the puppy's ear. "That's Samnang. That's the human we are here to help. As Love Puppies, it's our job to help kids in need."

The little pup looked around, sniffing and checking the new place out. It was clear that he didn't quite understand what was going on.

Which might have been a good thing for the puppy team, because at that very moment, and right at the start of this new mission, the pups already felt like they were failing. If something happened to Samnang right in front of their eyes—that would be bad news!

It also wouldn't make them very good at this

task of teaching the newbie how to successfully help human children.

"I don't want them to hurt him, Rosie," Noodles urged the team leader. "We've got to do something."

But Rosie's mind raced. She could feel her own puppy heart pound in her chest. Noodles's nose glowed, and the worry from Clyde and Barkley filled the air. What could they do without being spotted? How could they help him before something really bad happened?

The blond one stepped even closer to Samnang, their noses almost touching.

"You think you're *so* smart, don't you, Pint-Size," he said.

"No, I don't, Richie. I promise I don't!" said Samnang, his voice scared and small. Samnang scrunched up his face with fear, shrugged his shoulders up to his ears, and closed his eyes tightly. "Please don't hurt me. I'm sorry. Whatever I did, I'm sorry."

"'Please don't hurt me,'" mocked the brown-haired kid in a high-pitched voice. "'I'm sorry, I'm sorry,'" he teased.

"Good one, Salvador," laughed Richie.

The puppies trembled from behind the shrub.

Just then, footsteps echoed from down the hallway, and the two bullies stepped backward and looked in the direction of the echo.

A teacher hurried past. Her eyes focused on a tablet's screen, which she flicked with her finger.

"Heading back to class, right, gentlemen?" she said, never lifting her eyes from the screen.

"Yes, Ms. Lizbeth," said Richie in a sweet voice. "We were just helping this kid find his class. He got lost or something."

"Mmhmm," she answered. "Class please," she repeated.

"This isn't finished, Pint-Size," said Salvador in a whisper, and he and Richie turned and walked away.

Samnang stood there for a second more, like he was glued to the wall. He slowed his fast breathing by inhaling deeply and wiped sweat from his forehead. Then he took off running in the opposite direction and disappeared around a corner.

The pups sat in complete silence. The scary situation played over and over again in their heads.

"That was just paw-ful," said Clyde in a tiny voice, breaking the silence.

The other pups nodded, all except for the baby puppy who barked a tiny, happy bark and wiggled his tail.

"I think we should get back," said Rosie.

"Yeah. And we're going to have to think of something fast," said Noodles. "There's no way we can let something like that happen to Samnang again!"

"I couldn't agree more," said Barkley.

"Paws in, Pups," said Rosie, her voice much less chipper than it usually was.

With the opening of the portal, an ache stung each of the puppies' hearts.

Why were those kids being so mean to Samnang? And what could this team of puppies do to stop them?

Chapter 4
Barking at Bullying

When the puppies touched down in the Love Puppy living room, Clyde prepared a bowl of kibble for the newbie. The rest of the team huddled beside the Bone.

"That was *not* good," Rosie reiterated. "Not good at all."

"I thought they were going to hit him for sure," said Noodles.

"Why were they doing that?" asked Clyde. "Why weren't they just being nice to him?"

Barkley sat quietly, staring at his paws. He sighed deeply.

"What is it, Pup?" asked Rosie.

"I know what that was," said Barkley. "I've heard of that kind of thing before—in a book I was reading one time. In the story, they called it *bullying.*"

"Bullying?" repeated Rosie. "I've never heard of that."

"Yeah," Barkley said with a nod. "It is a terrible thing."

"Bullying. Hmmm. Let's learn more!" Rosie turned to face the Crystal Bone and placed her paws on it. "Bone, what is bullying?"

The Bone began to flash, and the word BULLYING shined across its surface. Rosie closed her eyes.

"Oh my," she said with a shudder. With her eyes still closed, she began to whimper.

"What is it?" called Noodles. "You can tell us!"

"It's terrible! Just terrible," said Rosie. She opened

her eyes and looked toward her puppy team. "Show them please, Bone."

A video flashed across the ceiling showing images of people. Some images showed a person yelling at another. Others showed people pushing and shoving, or ripping things and breaking them. Often, the pictures showed someone doing awful things to someone else.

Each of the puppies covered their eyes like it was a scary movie but sneaked peeks at the video here and there.

"Bone said bullying is something dreadful humans can do to each other. It's when one or even more people are mean to each other just because they want to come off as powerful or strong." More images flashed as Rosie continued to speak. "And Bone also said bullies look for others to be mean to so they can say and do hurtful things to them."

The Bone turned on the sound, and the puppies listened as hurtful words filled the Doghouse.

Just then, the baby puppy dashed over and began barking at the video. He barked and barked and bared his teeth at the ceiling.

"Whoa," said Rosie. "It's okay, little guy. It's just a video." She padded over to him and gently patted his head, pulling him into a hug.

The video clicked off and all was silent, except for the little puppy's growls still aimed at the ceiling.

"Don't worry. It's off now." Rosie said, still patting him gently as he nuzzled into her neck, calming down. "This little guy didn't like that, huh? And for good reason. Bullying is bad!"

Rosie turned her attention to her team of puppies, who still covered their eyes with their paws.

"You can look now," she said, her voice tender and soft.

Noodles, Barkley, and Clyde slowly uncovered their eyes.

"That was the worst thing I've ever seen," said Barkley. "Way worse than the book I read."

"Yeah. It's awful. And an even sadder thing is, Bone said that usually, bullies are people who are hurting, too. So they hurt others to make themselves feel better." Rosie stood, still holding the puppy, who had clearly grown even bigger since they got home. "You're growing so fast, huh?" she said, carrying him back over to his doggie bowl so he could finish his dinner.

"Well, I didn't like that one bit," said Barkley.

"Me neither," said Noodles. "If that kind of thing happened to me, I would cry and cry and never want to go to school."

"But Samnang *has* to go to school," said Clyde. "How else will he learn? How will he make friends? And how will he get even better at all the school stuff he's already super good at?"

"You've hit it right on the nose, Clydie," said Rosie. "This is another reason why we need to help him! Nobody deserves to be treated that way, especially not at school. And nobody deserves to live in fear of being hurt."

"We've got to do something and soon!" said Barkley.

This mission was truly turning out to be a tough one.

Chapter 5
A Dynamite Name

"What to do, what to do?" asked Rosie as she paced

back and forth in front of the Crystal Bone. She

stopped mid-step and turned to Barkley. "What

did the characters do in the story you read, Barkley?

The one that told you about bullying?"

"Well, they all had magical powers, so they used those to stop the bullies. But I don't think that will help Samnang in his situation."

"True," said Rosie. "We all know humans don't have magic." She paced a few more times. "Well, Pups, what would you do if someone was treating you like that?"

"I would tell them to stop," said Noodles.

"Yeah," added Clyde. "Tell them stop in a big voice, like LEAVE ME ALONE!" shouted Clyde at the top of his puppy lungs. His voice bounced off the walls, causing the little puppy to cry out and leap into the air. His paw pads began to glow gold, and as soon as he landed back on the ground, he took off running at full speed.

And run he did! The puppy zipped and flashed back and forth across the living room, crashing into tables and causing papers and doggie toys to fly everywhere. He bumped into walls, causing Rosie's flowerpots to fall from their shelves and windowsills. Soil and flowers were soon all over the floor.

But the little puppy didn't stop there. He kept going, dashing at lightning speed and yapping as he went.

By now, the banner-pups joined in on the commotion, barking and jumping on their hanging banners. Even the little version of the new puppy wiggled and barked from its golden flag.

"We've got to calm him down," shouted Rosie

over the ruckus, "before he destroys the whole headquarters!"

The Love Puppy team launched into action. Clyde flew through the air, trying to keep up with the pup. But the little puppy was just too fast. Each time Clyde dove down to catch him, the pup zipped from one space to another.

Next, Noodles dropped some rain puddles onto the floor and froze them over. But instead of sliding to a stop, the pup picked up even more speed, his fast feet warming up the ice and melting it back into water, causing him to splash all across the floor.

Rosie used her powers to grow giant vines that reached out for the puppy like arms. But with each zip and zoom, the branches got more and more tangled as they reached for him until they were a green mess of viny knots.

"I've got it!" called Barkley. He morphed into a large, purple butterfly net and swooped the little puppy up. Then he morphed back into his body, holding the puppy tightly, rocking him and whispering, "It's okay, boy. It's okay. I've got you. I've got you."

The puppy whimpered, his legs still moving at lightning speed, a dull golden light illuminating the air. With Barkley's soft voice and gentle pats, the puppy's legs slowed to a stop. He leaned into Barkley's fur and fell right to sleep wrapped up in Barkley's warm paws.

The Love Puppy team looked around at the disaster in their living room: water, soil, plants, papers, and toys!

"Well, it definitely looks like something exploded in here," said Rosie with a chuckle. "Let's put this little guy to bed and get it cleaned up while we think of how to help Samnang tomorrow."

"He can sleep in my room," said Barkley. "We can use his basket as a bed." As Barkley began carrying the sleeping pooch away, he stopped and said, "Hey, we never gave him a name. What should we call this little ball of energy?"

"Good point, Barkley Boy," said Rosie. "We did

forget to name him. What should we call him?"

"I know," said Clyde. "How about Kibble, since he loves to eat kibble?"

"That could work," said Rosie with a laugh. "But I don't know if he'd want to be named after food. That's like calling you Cupcake-Clyde."

"Hmm," replied Clyde. "More like Chicken-Fried-Steak-Clyde. Mmmmmm," he said, picturing a huge, oversized chicken-fried steak in his head.

"Lightning?" asked Noodles. "Since he's quick as a flash?" she said while a spark of lightning jolted across her puppy palms.

"Maybe," said Rosie, "especially now that we know his power is superspeed."

"But he's pretty feisty, too," added Clyde. "You saw how he went after that video with all the bullies."

Each of the puppies shuddered, thinking about the horrible video they had watched.

"I've got it," said Barkley. "Dynamite! He's quick as a flashing blast, a ball full of energy and spunk, and able to make a Love Puppy living room look like the site of a firecracker frenzy. So . . . Dynamite!"

"That's perfect!" said Rosie. The others yipped in agreement.

"Good night, little Dynamite," whispered Barkley as he carried the snoozing pup down the hall and into his bedroom. "Sleep tighty-tight."

Chapter 6
Foul Play on the B-ball Court

After Dynamite was put to bed and the living room was back in order, the pups sat around the table eating dinner and discussing the mission.

"I liked the idea of speaking up and saying stop," said Barkley. "Something like that might help."

"How would we help Samnang do that, though?" asked Rosie. "A note, maybe?" Notes had been helpful in many of their previous missions.

"Maybe," answered Noodles. "What about if he just walked away? Like when he sees those bullies, he just goes the other way?"

"That could work!" said Barkley. "That's what we can do to help. If we position ourselves just right, anytime those two bullies are near him, we can use our magic to help him to avoid them."

"Yes, avoiding," exclaimed Rosie. "I think that just might do it! Let's give it a try bright and early tomorrow morning."

* * *

The next morning, with Dynamite all rested and happy again—he was at least two times bigger now than when he first arrived—and every puppy's tummy filled with a yummy breakfast, the pups found Samnang as he walked to school.

"No bullies here," Barkley whispered as they hid behind a Rosie-grown rosebush along the way.

They also didn't see the bullies during breakfast in the cafeteria, or anytime that morning.

"So far, so good," Noodles said. When the recess bell rang, the Love Puppy team hid behind an empty trashcan.

"There he is," said Clyde as Samnang hurried

from his classroom. "He's moving as fast as Dynamite does."

It was true: Samnang power walked past the blacktop, looking over his shoulder again and again. As he reached the edge of the blacktop, he seemed to glue his eyes to a door a few feet away.

"The library," said Rosie, reading the words above the door he stared at. "He's going to the library! Maybe he's already trying to avoid them."

"Good thinking, Samnang!" said Barkley. "Just like we had said, avoiding a bully is a great solution. That way, they can't bother you if they can't get to you!"

"And," added Noodles, "I bet there's an adult in

there. Having an adult nearby can help keep a bully from bullying you, too!"

"I think Samnang may have figured those things out for himself," said Rosie. "Maybe he doesn't need us after all."

But just before Samnang made it to the library entrance, Richie and Salvador popped out of nowhere and blocked his path.

"Where did they even come from?" asked Clyde.

That didn't matter now because avoiding them was no longer something Samnang could do.

Richie moved right into Samnang's space while holding a basketball in his hands.

Samnang's brown skin seemed to lighten

with fear. He swallowed hard, bowed his head, and looked toward the ground instead of in Richie's eyes.

"Oh, hey, Richie. Hey, Salvador," he finally said in a shaky voice, more to the ground than to the boys.

"Wanna play basketball?" said Richie, shoving the ball into Samnang's stomach as Salvador looked around, checking for teachers.

"No thank you," answered Samnang with more breath than voice, doubled over from the impact of the ball. "I actually have somewhere to—"

"Sure you do," said Salvador, moving in close. He put his arm around Samnang's shoulders and turned him toward the basketball court. Both boys outsized Samnang like an ant next to grasshoppers.

Samnang tried to wiggle free, but this only caused Salvador to hold on to his shoulders even tighter. The look on Samnang's face made it clear to the puppies that he was close to tears.

"What are they going to do to him?" whispered Barkley.

Richie and Salvador led Samnang to the basketball court, and the pups watched as the bullies separated the group of boys there into teams. Richie, Salvador, and another kid versus Samnang and two other small boys.

Then the pups watched in horror as the game

began. Richie bumped and pushed Samnang, snatching the ball and causing him to fall over and over again.

Salvador tripped and shoved Samnang, but the other kids continued to play as if they didn't see any of it—although, they were sure to keep their distance from the big bullies on the court.

"Why won't anyone do anything to help him?" cried Clyde.

"I think they're scared, too," said Noodles.

"Somebody's *got* to do something. This is the worst!" yelled Rosie.

A recess duty teacher came over. "Are we playing nicely over here?" she asked, looking at Samnang.

"Yes, Ms. Winn," chimed Richie with syrup in his voice. He high-fived Samnang, then turned back to the teacher. "See?!"

"Okay. Just don't be too rough, please," she said, walking back to her post.

This time, avoiding hadn't worked. And the bullies were too good at pretending to be nice, fooling any adult who asked. But the puppies' hearts broke with each bump and push Samnang took.

What else could they do to help this bullied kid in need?

Chapter 7
How to Help?

The pups continued watching, wincing every time Samnang was hit.

"Do you see this, little guy?" whispered Barkley in Dynamite's ear. "This is what we do: We watch and figure out how to assist kids like Samnang. But right now, we are at a loss for what to do to help."

Dynamite whimpered a little bit as he watched. "Help," he muttered.

"Yes! How to help," said Barkley. "I think he's getting it."

"And he said his first word!" added Rosie. *Help* was a good first word to say. She eyed the not-so-tiny puppy who had grown even bigger.

When the bell finally rang, Samnang was out of breath and exhausted. He moved away from the team of bullies who high-fived and laughed.

Just then, another kid walked by.

"Look, it's Dumbo the Giant," said Richie, pointing to a tall boy who hurried past, heading to his class's recess line. When the boy saw them moving in his direction, he picked up his step and tripped over his own feet, landing hard. Immediately, tears welled up and ran down the kid's brown cheeks. He rocked side to side on the ground and shook his hands quickly in front of his chest.

"Ooooh! Dumbo falls hard!" yelled Salvador as he and Richie stood over him.

"Look! He's trying to fly away!" added Richie.

Salvador pretended to throw the ball at the kid, causing the other boy to tense up as he rocked on the ground. This made the bullies laugh even harder.

"Time to head to class," yelled a voice over whistles being blown.

The bullies left the boy on the ground and walked away.

The puppies watched as Samnang rushed over to the boy and extended a hand. Even though Samnang was so much smaller, he used all his might to help the kid up.

"Thanks," mumbled the other boy, not making eye contact with Samnang.

"No problem," Samnang said. The two of them walked next to each other in silence toward their separate classroom lines.

Finally, Samnang said, "I'm Samnang. I'm in the second grade."

"Mandeep," said the other boy.

"Well, see ya around, Mandeep."

"Bye."

The boys parted and joined their lines.

From behind the trashcan, the pups huddled together with Dynamite in the middle.

"Those bullies are the absolute worst," said Rosie.

"And they're not just mean to Samnang. They're mean to others, too. Like that boy Mandeep."

"I wish we could teach *them* a lesson," said Barkley with bite in his voice.

"But our mission is to help Samnang," reminded Noodles. "And I have no idea of what to do! But whatever it is, I can't sit back and watch Samnang get pummeled again like that. We've got to do something next time!"

"Well, trying to avoid the bullies could work. But, just like we saw, it won't work all the time."

"Yeah," added Clyde. "And trying to ignore them could work, too, but not if they are too close that they are in your space—like they were today."

"I still think adults are a solution, here. I think he needs to tell someone," said Barkley. "A teacher, a coach, a librarian. An adult who he can trust and who can help."

"Speaking up about what is happening—that's a solid idea!" said Rosie. "Now to figure out how to do it."

"Let's go on an adult hunt!" said Clyde. That was another great idea—and in the past, going on hunts for friends had proven successful for the puppy team.

The pups hurried behind the classroom that they saw Samnang go into. They peeked inside a back window and saw him working with a group.

"What about his teacher? He seems nice," said Noodles, observing the teacher as he paid Samnang a compliment.

"That's a good idea. Do you think that would be enough?" asked Rosie.

"Maybe he could tell more adults, just in case. Who's the boss of a school?" asked Clyde.

"The principal!" answered Barkley.

"And there are some adults in the lunchroom, right? And in the library and on the playgrounds, too. Maybe we should tell all of them!" Noodles said.

"Pups! We know what to do," said Rosie. "Let's head back to headquarters and get some letters pup-pared!"

Chapter 8
A Lunchtime Connection

After getting back to headquarters and typing out copies of the letters using Typewriter-Barkley, the pups found themselves back outside Samnang's classroom just as the lunch bell rang.

They watched as Samnang's eyes found Mandeep in the lunch line.

"Hi, Mandeep," he said. "Want to eat lunch with me in the library? Mr. Burton always lets me help him organize the books."

"Okay," said Mandeep.

"I'll let the cafeteria teacher know. She lets me go." Samnang then leaned in and whispered in a voice that the pups could barely hear. "It also means Richie and Salvador will leave us alone. They never go to the library."

With the mention of the bullies, Mandeep shook his head and waved his hands a little, even though Richie and Salvador were out of sight.

"I don't like those guys," Mandeep said, never looking at Samnang.

"I just wish they'd leave me—well, *us*—alone," added Samnang. "Maybe if you and I hang out together more . . . maybe they will. You like to solve puzzles, right? I've seen you working on some at recess sometimes."

"Yeah," answered Mandeep.

"Cool. Me too. And I have this cool puzzle book my brother gave me—that's why I brought my backpack," he said, motioning to the bag slung over his shoulder. "I'll show you it when we get to the library."

The boys continued their conversation as they

entered the cafeteria, out of earshot for the puppies.

"Well, it surely seems like Samnang is good about thinking of ways to avoid those bullies," said Barkley. "And he's good at making new friends."

The other pups nodded their heads.

"I like how he's also thinking ahead about things that might make those bullies leave him alone— like hanging out with Mandeep so they wouldn't have to face them alone," said Noodles.

"It is definitely a good start," said Rosie.

Dynamite yipped happily and said, "Good."

"Yes, boy," replied Clyde, "this is something *good*!"

"I still think the letters are a good idea, too. Just

in case," said Rosie. Covering as many bases as possible when it came to bullies seemed like a good idea to the pups.

Samnang and Mandeep walked out of the cafeteria together, holding their trays. They were still chatting away about things they liked.

"Hey," said Samnang, "I've got to go to the bathroom first. Will you take my tray to the library with you? I'll meet you there in a second."

"Okay," said Mandeep, taking Samnang's tray.

"See you there!" said Samnang, speedwalking toward a bathroom. He looked around and over his shoulder as he hurried away.

"Now seems like the perfect time to slip the

letters into his bag," said Rosie. "When he sees them, he'll know who to give them to, since we put the adults' names on each," Rosie said proudly.

"We thought of everything," added Noodles.

Rosie placed the folded letters between her teeth, and the puppies tried to quietly follow behind Samnang.

"He's walking too fast to put these in his backpack," called Barkley. "Maybe we should just deliver them ourselves, that way—" But just as he was finishing his sentence, Dynamite snatched one of the letters from Rosie's jaws and dashed down the hallway in Samnang's direction. As he ran, his paw pads glowed golden and bright.

The pups stopped and gasped, watching Dynamite zoom through the walkway, in plain sight of humans. Then Dynamite disappeared around the corner.

"Oh no!" cried Barkley. "He's going to be seen!"

Chapter 9
Who Wrote This?

"Come on, Pups," shouted Barkley. "We're going

to lose him!" Barkley morphed into an invisible

Blanket-Barkley and draped himself over the

pups. Then, as fast as their puppy legs could

go—but not even close to Dynamite's speed—

they charged after their little puppy pal.

"Wait! Listen," said Noodles. "Can you hear that?"

Down a separate hallway, the team could hear the echo of Dynamite's barks. The puppies hurried down a row of classrooms, still hidden by Barkley. Then they turned to find the library.

Samnang kneeled down and petted Dynamite, who barked with delight and wagged his tail gleefully.

"Where did you come from, little guy?" asked Samnang. "And what is this?" Samnang picked up a folded sheet of paper that was at Dynamite's feet and opened it.

"'Dear Principal Rigsby,'" Samnang read aloud. "'My name is Samnang and I am being bullied by two boys: Richie and Salvador.'" Samnang gasped and continued. "'They push me and are mean to me and I don't know what to do. Please help.'" Samnang looked around. "Who wrote this? Where did this come from—"

"There you are, Pint-Size," said Richie, stepping out from around the corner, followed by Salvador. "Thought you were going to hide away in your little library before you gave us your money?"

Samnang dropped the paper and scooped up Dynamite, holding him protectively. Dynamite bared his teeth and growled.

"What's that?" asked Salvador, pointing at Dynamite. "Looks like a blown-up potato. Is that your lunch for today?" The boys cackled.

"Wait, what's *that* and why's it got my name on it?" asked Richie. He reached down and picked up the sheet of paper, reading it silently. Then his face turned bright red, and he crumpled the sheet up in his fist. He glared at Samnang, his piercing blue eyes seeming to cut right through him.

Then he rammed his right fist into his own open palm.

Uh-oh! This wasn't going to be good.

Chapter 10
A Mighty Showdown

Samnang gulped and stepped back, pushing up against the wall and hugging Dynamite.

"It's okay, little guy," he whispered as he gently rubbed the small corgi.

"So, you thought you were going to rat us out,

huh?" Richie said, closing the space between him and Samnang.

Dynamite began growling louder than ever before. He leapt out of Samnang's arms and landed on the floor. Then he ran circles around Salvador and Richie, barking and nipping at their calves, causing them to step away from Samnang.

"Whoa," whispered Barkley. "Look at him go!"

Dynamite barked and barked, the sound of his voice circling the boys as he dashed, wrapping them in barks.

"Get your crazy dog, Pint-Size," yelled Salvador, fear all over his face. "I hate dogs. I got bit when I was five. That's where I got this," he said, pointing at a scar on his cheek. "I HATE DOGS!"

Salvador's words caused the hidden puppy team to growl, too, from their hiding place.

"Chill out, man, it's just a little runt dog," Richie said, fear coloring his voice. "We can just kick it over. Easy." But even with his tough words, Richie stayed in his spot like his own feet were glued to the ground, his head moving as he tried to keep his eyes on the speedy puppy.

Dynamite stopped in his tracks, facing the two bullies with Samnang behind him. Dynamite took two steps back, showing his teeth, preparing to lunge their way.

Just then, Noodles's voice carried on the wind

and whispered into Dynamite's ear so only he could hear her. She whispered, "Bark on three, Dynamite. Bark on three: One, two, THREE!"

And on three, Dynamite barked with all his might, along with the rest of the Love Puppy team hidden around the corner. All their barks mixed together, echoing throughout the hallway like it was filled with invisible ghost dogs, yapping away. Noodles kicked up a static wind that blasted at the boys and caused Dynamite's fur to stand up on end, making him look like he grew in size.

Richie's and Salvador's eyes bulged, staring at the growing pooch with the giant voice. They pedaled back away from Dynamite and then took off running in the opposite direction. Dynamite lunged forward a few feet in the direction they ran, continuing to bark.

The quiet returned to the hallway.

Samnang let out a breath and bent over to pet Dynamite, who licked his hand.

"Thank you, little guy," he said. "You're so small, but you totally saved me."

Noodles's voice took to her wind again and whispered, "Time to go, Dynamite."

Dynamite jumped up and licked Samnang's cheek. Then he dashed away like lightning, retreating beneath Blanket-Barkley's invisible shield.

"That was amazing, Dynamite!" said Rosie. She and the others hurried back the way they came and hid behind a bush outside. They hugged and kissed Dynamite and ruffled his fur.

"That was such a mighty thing to do, Dynamite," said Barkley.

"Might-ee," repeated Dynamite.

"Yes! Mighty," Barkley responded. "That nickname fits perfectly! And you know what, Mighty," Barkley said with a giant smile, "I think you've just helped us complete our mission."

Or so he thought.

Chapter 11
Better Together

Back at the Doghouse, the puppies kicked back in a puppy heap, their tummies full from the dinner they just ate.

After the lunchtime showdown, the pups had stayed at school to watch Samnang as he finished the day and walked home. And for the entire time, Richie and Salvador were nowhere to be found.

"You know, Barkley, I think you are right," said Rosie, smiling at Dynamite who rested on Barkley. "I think this Mighty guy here *has* solved our bullying problem."

"Job well done, Mighty," said Clyde, rubbing the puppy's head. Dynamite had grown even more and was now the size of the other Love Puppies.

"Yeah," added Noodles, "and we didn't even have to deliver any of the letters—though telling an adult was a great idea."

"But I do think we should go back tomorrow and check," said Rosie. "Just to be sure."

"Deal," agreed the pups. And they shuffled off to bed, so they'd be all rested for tomorrow.

* * *

The next day, the pups hid in their usual spot for recess. They watched as Samnang left his class. But this time, he didn't hurry toward the library, looking over his shoulders or watching his feet. Instead, he walked with his head held high and he headed straight for the playground.

The pups looked around. Where were Richie and Salvador?

"There!" shouted Barkley.

On the blacktop, the boys stared up at Mandeep, who kept his eyes on the ground. Richie poked

Mandeep's chest with his index finger and Salvador smacked the basketball that he held loudly with his palm.

"I don't want to play," whispered Mandeep. "I don't want to play. I don't want to play," he whispered repeatedly, his eyes still looking down.

"You're playing because we said you're playing," said Salvador, stepping toward Mandeep.

Mandeep stepped back. Tears welled up in his eyes.

"And don't try to run. You're not even fast. We'll catch you, easy," said Richie.

"Hey!" a loud voice rang out. "Leave him alone!"

The puppies recognized the voice instantly,

though this was the loudest they had ever heard it. They turned to find the person who spoke up and watched as he advanced toward the bullies.

"He said he doesn't want to play," said the voice, loud but still just a bit shaky. "Just leave him alone."

"Well, if it isn't itty-bitty Pint-Size trying to man up," said Richie, who was now facing Samnang.

"Yeah, I'm small," said Samnang. "So what!"

"Ha!" said Salvador. "What are *you* gonna do?"

At this, Dynamite's fur bristled, and he began growling lowly, teeth bared.

"Hold on, Mighty-Might," said Rosie. "Let's see what happens. That's what we do. We watch and help if we're needed."

"You gonna sic your weirdo runt dog on us again?" continued Salvador.

"Maybe!" Samnang retorted.

Salvador's eyes widened and he looked around as if in search of the firecracker dog.

"Or maybe I'll just scream loud enough so the recess duty teacher can hear me," said Samnang. His voice was even and confident. More confident than the puppies had ever heard from him—and it made them smile and wag their tails like they did at Barkley's charades noodle dance.

Samnang stood his ground and looked right up into Richie's eyes. "Whatever I do, I'm not scared of you anymore. You just bully anybody who doesn't stand up to you. Well, *I'm* standing up to you. Hit me if you want to, but he doesn't want to play with you. And neither do I!"

Richie's face crinkled up with anger. He took one step closer to Samnang.

"I don't want to play with you either," said one of the other kids who always played basketball on the bullies' team.

"Me neither," said another.

"None of us do," added another, each kid joining behind Samnang, even Mandeep.

Suddenly, Samnang, Mandeep, and a handful of other kids *all* stood up tall, facing Richie and Salvador. Even though most of the other kids were small, and Salvador and Richie towered over them, the bullies didn't say a word. They just eyed the kids angrily, looking at each of their faces as they stood behind Samnang.

And each of the kids looked determined and sure. No fear. No concern. Just unified where they stood.

"Yeah, whatever," Richie finally said. "We don't want to play with you losers, anyway." And then, Richie and Salvador turned and walked away.

Samnang smiled and let out a breath.

"It worked!" whispered Barkley. "Pushing down his fear, using his voice, and finally standing up to those bullies really worked!"

"Thanks, man," said one of the other kids. "We hated playing with them but . . ." The kid's voice trailed off and he didn't finish the sentence. He just folded his arms and looked away.

It was clear that Richie and Salvador had scared everybody else, too, especially if they had to stand up to them by themselves.

"You guys want to play soccer? I think they have an extra ball over there," said Samnang.

"Yeah," the other kids agreed.

"I'll watch," said Mandeep.

"Okay," said Samnang. And all of them walked off together.

"How did you get so brave all of a sudden? To

stand up to them like that?" asked Mandeep.

"I don't know. I just got tired of being bullied," said Samnang. "And yesterday, something reminded me that even if you are small—like me—you can still act big."

"Oh, like small but mighty?" said Mandeep.

"Exactly. Like small but mighty."

Chapter 12
Small, But Oh-So-Mighty

Back home at the Love Puppy Headquarters, the puppies darted around the backyard.

"Tag!" shouted Rosie as she touched Barkley with an open paw.

Barkley giggled and then turned in Dynamite's

direction. "I'm gonna get you, Mighty," he called, sprinting toward the corgi. Dynamite dashed away going this way and that like a flash of fur and golden light.

"You're too fast, boy," chuckled Noodles.

The whole team turned toward Dynamite and yelled, "Puppy pile!" Dynamite yipped and sat on his bottom as the team descended on him, piling on top of him, covering him in puppy kisses and laughing.

"Pup-ee pile. Pup-ee pile," he said.

"His talking is getting better and better," shouted Barkley. "Good boy!"

Dynamite barked with excitement. Each puppy smiled at him with affection.

"You really saved the day, little guy," said Rosie.

"Yeah," added Clyde, "and on a really hard mission. Having to figure out how to deal with a bully was not easy at all!"

All the puppies agreed.

Rosie added, "Not easy, but so important. Watching Samnang showed me that."

"Uh-huh," said Noodles, "and that if there is someone bullying you, you don't have to take it. Instead, there are things you can do. Like ignore them or avoid them."

"And if that doesn't work, you can always tell an adult you trust. That adult can help!" said Clyde.

"You also have to push down your emotions,"

Noodles said, letting her nose flash. "When those bullies saw fear or crying, it made them act even worse."

"So true," said Rosie. "Like if you let the bully know they are getting to you, it makes them meaner and scarier."

"Mm-hmm," responded Noodles.

"But what's *super* important is that you've got to act brave and stand up for yourself. And for others. Just like Mighty did."

"Might-ee," repeated Dynamite.

"Yes! Mighty. Just like you," said Barkley.

"And not just that," said Rosie. "You showed Samnang that even though he may be small, he can be mighty, too. That was pup-tastic, how he stood up for himself and Mandeep. That helped all the other kids join in, too. You, little pup, are small, but oh-so-mighty!"

At that moment, the Crystal Bone began playing the new melody again, which sang through the window and out on the wind.

"Welp," said Rosie, "the Crystal Bone calls." She and the pups hurried back into the house with Mighty leading the way. When they got to the Bone, it flashed gold. Rosie placed her paws on the surface to receive the message.

"I've got some good news and some bad news," she said, with a heavy sigh. "Bone said we completed our mission and our first training task—helping Samnang and showing Mighty the ropes of how to be a Love Puppy."

"Yip yip hooray for Mighty!" the pups cheered.

"You are officially on the Love Puppy team," said Barkley. "Wait . . . but what's the bad news?"

"Well, since we've taught him a lot about what we do, now he must go out into our world and begin a new Love Puppy team. That way, he and his team can help even *more* kids." There was sadness in Rosie's voice as she shared the news.

All the other puppies whimpered and surrounded Mighty, hugging him closely.

"But he's still so little," said Barkley.

"Yes, but big enough to go out on his own—like us!" said Rosie.

"We're going to miss you, boy," said Clyde. "You're one tough cookie!"

"Thank you for joining us on our mission and for showing us what you can do," said Noodles.

"We learned just as much from you as you did from us," added Rosie.

Barkley dragged Dynamite's basket from his bedroom and over to the group. Then they all headed back outside to the front door where they had first met Mighty.

"Don't forget us, Small-But-Oh-So-Mighty Dynamite," said Barkley.

Mighty climbed into the basket. He looked at each pup. "Ro-see," he said. "Noo-dles, Cly-dee, Bark-lee. Thank you. You pup-tastic!"

With a gold light shimmering around Mighty and the basket, the Crystal Bone played the melody.

Just like that, a portal opened and Mighty disappeared into it, vanishing from sight.

"That was one special pup," said Barkley. "I hope we'll get to see him again."

The others yipped their agreement.

"I'm sad to see him go," said Rosie, "but I'm happy to hear that more Love Puppies around the world will be able to help kids in need."

"Me too," chimed the puppies.

"Let's head in for a snack," said Clyde.

The Love Puppy team ambled back inside with the idea of more kids getting the help they needed swirling around in their hearts.

Isn't that such a magical idea? Not just pups helping kids, like the Love Puppies do, but kids helping kids, too? Like Samnang and Mandeep?

That's the power you hold—the power to stand up to bullies and help others.

And that's pretty magical indeed!

Read all of the Love Puppies' paw-some adventures!

SCHOLASTIC
scholastic.com

LOVEPUPPIES

Want more Love Puppy magic?

Read on for a sneak peek at their first adventure!

Chapter 1
Early Morning Message

Buzz, buzz! Buzz, buzz!

Rosie's doggie ears perked up at the sound that buzzed from down the hall of the Love Puppy Doghouse. She knew exactly what it was: the Crystal Bone. Her excellent ears could hear it vibrate. She could also see that it was flashing like crazy. Its blinking alert lit up the dim morning, even though it was all the way in the living room.

"Uh-oh," she said to herself. "The sun is not even up yet. Must be important." Rosie hopped out of her comfy doggie bed and bounded across the floor. Sleep would have to wait.

But just as she reached the door, something stopped her. A tickle or an itch—right in her chest, where her heart beat. She sat on her hind legs and looked down. A faint light seemed to shine ever so slightly beneath her fur. It shimmered for just a moment. Then it was gone.

That was strange, Rosie thought, gently touching

her chest with the front of her paw. Then the *buzz, buzz* of the Crystal Bone reminded Rosie she had a job to do. She shook the strange glow from her mind and raced into the hallway.

"Rise and shine, Love Puppies," she called. Not one of the other pups stirred.

Rosie tried again. "Upsy-daisy," she said, a little louder this time, "we've got an urgent message waiting!"

"All right, all right," said Barkley the dachshund, stretching his short legs. "I'm up."

"Great," said Rosie as she wagged her tail. Barkley and the rest of the puppies dragged themselves out of their rooms and down the hallway.

"This couldn't wait?" Noodles, the labradoodle, asked as she slouched past Rosie. "I was having the best dream ever. It was a beautiful day and there were rainbows and sunrays crisscrossing the sky!" Noodles wore a long nightcap that hung from her ears. It had a fuzzy ball on the very end.

"You know, even magical pups like us need our beauty sleep," whined Clyde, the Shar-Pei puppy, as he flew sleepily through the air. He yawned so widely that he almost bumped into the wall before landing on the rug in the main living room.

"I know, I know. But when the Crystal Bone calls, that means we've got work to do!" Rosie hurried into the living room after the other pups.

Each wall in the living room had large windows covered by paw-printed curtains. Small pots of beautiful flowers decorated each windowsill. Rosie had grown them herself. As she padded past them, the flowers opened and leaned toward her as if they were waving hello.

This was the Love Puppy Den: an enchanted place perfect for four magical pups to eat, sleep, play, and make plans to help kids in need! Along the walls hung four giant banners, each with a moving picture of one of the Love Puppies showing off their special magic—and in their signature colors.

Rosie and her soft golden fur stood out on the bright pink banner. She was a golden retriever with flower magic, the power to grow plants and flowers whenever she wanted.

A blue banner showed Clyde, a wrinkly Shar-Pei with the ability to fly. He didn't even need a cape!

The orange banner showcased Noodles, a shaggy labradoodle with the power to control weather and its different elements.

And the purple banner displayed Barkley, a tiny dachshund who could transform into anything he pleased!

These Love Puppies had hearts of gold, and helping human kids was their favorite thing to do. Even if it meant waking up earlier than usual.

The banner-pups jumped up at the sight of the real Love Puppies entering the room. They wiggled and danced across the walls. Noodles waved to her look-alike, and blew a gentle wind, causing each of the banners to flutter in her breeze. All the banner-pups yipped with excitement.

Clyde let out another gigantic yawn.

"Still sleepy?" asked Barkley. "I can help!" The heart-shaped pads on his paws glowed bright purple. Instantly, his long body morphed into a bright purple pillow.

"Paw-fect!" yipped Noodles. She and Clyde snuggled next to their Pillow-Barkley with a sigh.

"Okay, we've got serious business," Rosie began. "A new mission!" The look in Rosie's brown eyes told them this would be an important one.

"In that case, we're all ears!" said Clyde.

Rosie hurried to the center of the room where the oversized Crystal Bone blinked pink, blue, orange, and purple. The giant bone flashed, buzzed, and floated in the air whenever there was an urgent message.

While flower magic was Rosie's thing, she also was the only pup who could receive messages from the Crystal Bone. It served as a magical window into the human world during times of need.

And with how brightly the magical beacon was blinking right now was certainly a time of need for someone, somewhere!

When Rosie reached the Crystal Bone, she stood on her hind legs, placed both paws on it, and closed her eyes. The heart-shaped pads on Rosie's paws glowed a brilliant pink and soon a glittering *whoosh* of wind filled the room. The glitter swirled around her and the pups, ruffling the banners and the picture-pups, too. They howled from their hanging fabric.

Then, as suddenly as it had begun, the wind stopped and all was quiet.

Rosie opened her eyes. "Oh dear," she said.

The other pups ran over to where she stood, including Barkley, who had transformed back into his pup body.

Rosie pulled her paws from the Crystal Bone, pads up, as if she was holding something special. A puff of glitter floated above her upturned paws, slowly transforming into a small pink hologram of a human girl. The pups watched as tears fell from the girl's eyes. She ran over to her mother, held her tightly, and cried some more.

"Oh no!" whined Barkley. His wet nose was so close to the hologram in Rosie's paws that he could almost touch it. "She looks so sad!"

A tiny rain cloud drizzled over Noodles's head.

The flowers lining the windows drooped a little bit. Clyde sniffed loudly.

The three pups huddled around Rosie and the tiny pink human. They whimpered and howled and slowly wagged their tails.

"Love Puppies," Rosie said, raising the hologram into the air. "This is Meiko, and she needs our help!"

THE SPROUT FAIRIES
Forever Fairies

Forever fairies . . . and forever friends!

READ THEM ALL!

DRAGON GIRLS

#1: Azmina the Gold Glitter Dragon

#2: Willa the Silver Glitter Dragon

#3: Naomi the Rainbow Glitter Dragon

#4: Mei the Ruby Treasure Dragon

#5: Aisha the Sapphire Treasure Dragon

#6: Quinn the Jade Treasure Dragon

**#7: Rosie the
Twilight Dragon**

**#8: Phoebe the
Moonlight Dragon**

**#9: Stella the
Starlight Dragon**

**#10: Grace the
Cove Dragon**

**#11: Zoe the
Beach Dragon**

**#12: Sofia the
Lagoon Dragon**

**#13: Hana the
Thunder Dragon**

**#14: Mina the
Lightning Dragon**

**#15: Zora the
Snow Dragon**

Collect them all!

DRAGON GAMES

PLAY THE GAME. SAVE THE REALM.

READ ALL OF TEAM DRAGON'S ADVENTURES!

Read about all of Kira's GREAT ideas!

WHERE EVERY PUPPY FINDS A HOME